D0605826

Pete the Cat

Saves Christmas

Art by
James Dean
(creator of Pete the Cat)

Story by
Eric Litwin

HARPER
An Imprint of HarperCollinsPublishers

WITHDRAWN

Pete the Cat Saves Christmas
Copyright © by James Dean (for the character of Pete the Cat)
Copyright © 2012 by James Dean and Eric Litwin
All rights reserved. Manufactured in China.
No part of this book may be used or reproduced in any manner whatsoever without written permission except in the case of brief quotations embodied in critical articles and reviews. For information address HarperCollins Children's Books, a division of HarperCollins Publishers, 195 Broadway, New York, NY 10007.
www.harpercollinschildrens.com

Library of Congress Cataloging-in-Publication Data

Litwin, Eric.

Pete the cat saves Christmas / created and illustrated by James Dean ; story by Eric Litwin. — 1st ed.

p. cm.

Summary: When Santa falls ill and Christmas may have to be canceled, Pete the cat saves the day.

ISBN 978-0-06-211062-6 (trade bdg.) — ISBN 978-0-06-211063-3 (lib. bdg.)

ISBN 978-0-06-287659-1 (special ed.) — ISBN 978-0-06-294516-7 (paper-over-board)

[1. Stories in rhyme. 2. Cats—Fiction. 3. Christmas—Fiction. 4. Santa Claus—Fiction.] I. Dean, James, date, ill. II. Title.

PZ8.3.L7387Pe 2012 2011052408

[E]—dc23 CIP

AC

The artist used pen and ink, with watercolor and acrylic paint on 300lb hot press paper to create the illustrations for this book.

Typography by Jeanne L. Hogle

19 20 21 22 23 SCP 20 19 18 17 16 15 14 13

❖

First Edition

To the Real Pete—the little kitten I brought home from the shelter. And also to my first cat, Slim, and to all the others. I wish I could be a cat too. And to Margaret Anastas, who like Santa believes that Pete can save Christmas.

—J.D.

To Rachel and Naomi, my sisters, for all the stories we dreamed up together.

—E.L.

'Twas the day before Christmas and Santa was ill.
In the cold winter wind he had caught a bad chill.

Will Christmas be canceled?
Will it come to that?
"Never!" cried Santa. "Let's call Pete the Cat!"

Santa asked Pete
to deliver the toys
to all the good girls
and to all the good boys.
SANTA

"I'll do it!" said Pete.
"And although I am small,
at Christmas we give,
so I'll give it my all."
SANTA

Give it your all, give it your all.
At Christmas we give,
so give it your all.

Pete jumped in his minibus and started to roll.

"Road trip!" cried Pete.
NORTH POLE
"First stop—the North Pole."

The reindeer were waiting to give Pete a tow,

so he packed up the presents and told them to go.

Then the minibus flew, just like in a movie.

Pete the Cat cried,

"This is totally

groovy!"

"I can do it!"

said Pete, "and although I am small,
at Christmas we give, so I'll give it my all."

Give it your all, give it your all.
At Christmas we give,
so give it your all.

As the children were sleeping all snug in their beds,

Pete and his reindeer appeared overhead.

Straight down the chimney Pete flew in a dash,
then back in his minibus quick as a flash.

Each time he delivered a holiday gift,
he crossed off a name written on Santa's list.

Santa's list was so big, and Pete felt so small.
But at Christmas we give, so he gave it his all.

Give it your all, give it your all.
At Christmas we give,
so give it your all.
MICHAEL
JACOB
MADISON
MATTHEW
PIPER
EMILY
SAVANNAH
SOPHIA
ERIC
EMMA
OLIVIA
JESSICA
TREY
DESTINY
JOSH
HELEN
DORSEY
KIM
JAMES
JACKIE
LOHN
LANNET
SARAH
GRACE
DAVI
R
F

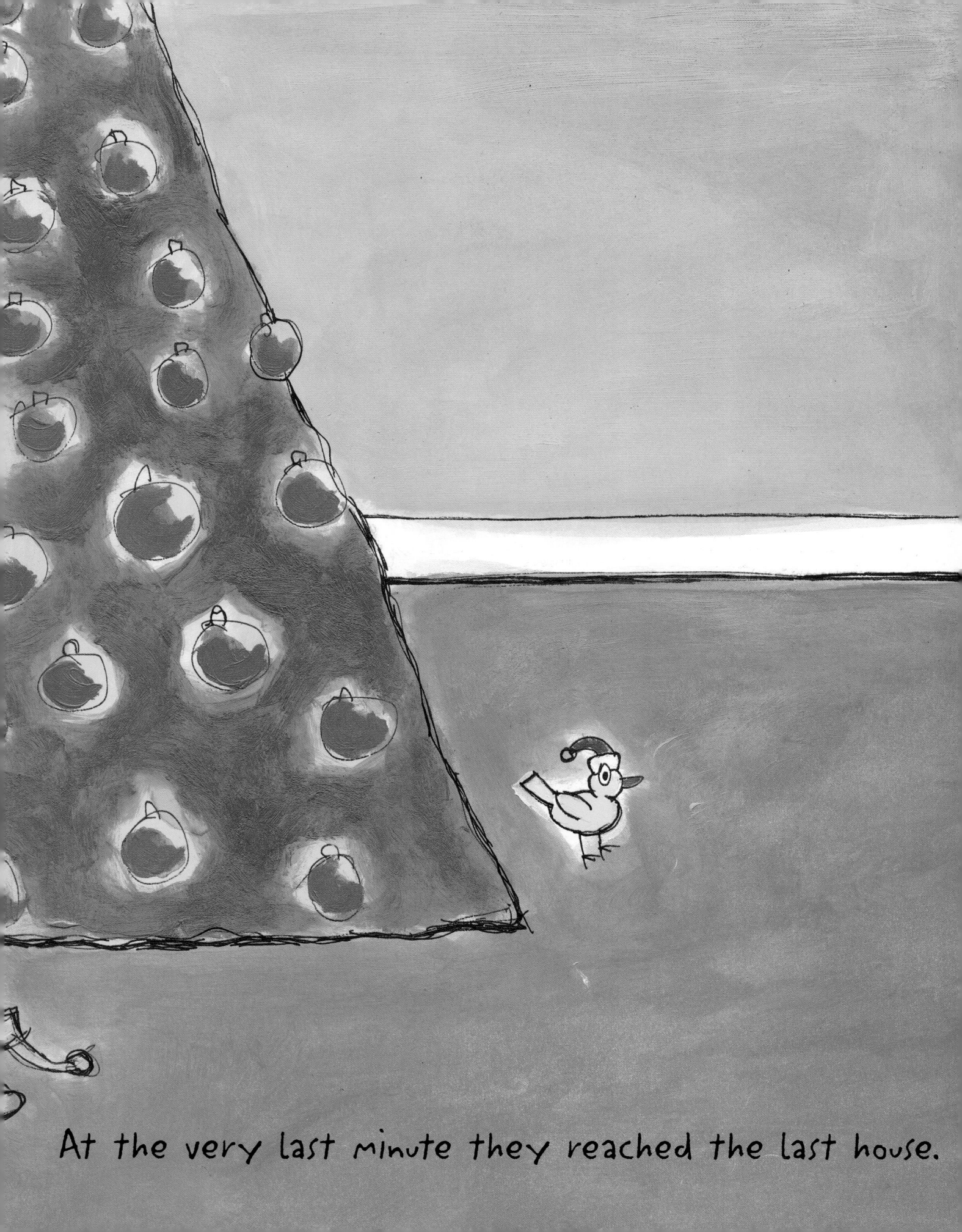

At the very last minute they reached the last house.

Pete dashed in and out just as quiet as a mouse.

Then right at the break of the new Christmas Day,

Pete and his reindeer were flying away.

NORTH POLE
TOYS INC.
SANTA
ELF

Back at the North Pole, old Santa was waiting.
The elves and the townsfolk were all celebrating.

Santa was dressed in his red coat and hat
and cried,

"Hip hip hurray for our

friend Pete the Cat."

"I did it!"

said Pete. "And although I am small,
in the spirit of Christmas I gave it my all!"

Give it your all, give it your all.
At Christmas we give,
so give it your all.
TO PETE

CONTRA COSTA COUNTY LIBRARY

31901065158679